NOVELLO CHORAL POPS

CW00448077

Published by

Novello Publishing Limited
part of The Music Sales Group
14-15 Berners Street, London W1T 3LJ, UK

Exclusive Distributors:

Music Sales Limited
Distribution Centre, Newmarket Road,
Bury St Edmunds, Suffolk IP33 3YB, UK

Music Sales Pty Limited
20 Resolution Drive,
Caringbah, NSW 2229, Australia

This book © Copyright 2009 Novello,

Unauthorised reproduction of any part of this
publication by any means including photocopying
is an infringement of copyright.

Edited by Rachel Lindley.
Music processed by Paul Ewers Music Design
and Camden Music.
Cover designed by Liz Barrand.

Printed in the EU

Your Guarantee of Quality
As publishers, we strive to produce every book
to the highest commercial standards.
The music has been freshly engraved and the
book has been carefully designed to minimise
awkward page turns and to make playing from
it a real pleasure.
Particular care has been given to specifying acid-free,
neutral-sized paper made from pulps which have not
been elemental chlorine bleached.
This pulp is from farmed sustainable forests and was
produced with special regard for the environment.
Throughout, the printing and binding have been
planned to ensure a sturdy, attractive publication
which should give years of enjoyment.
If your copy fails to meet our high standards,
please inform us and we will gladly replace it.

www.musicsales.com

FIELDS OF GOLD

WORDS & MUSIC BY STING

Arranged by Jonathan Wikeley

© Copyright 1992 Steerpike Limited/Steerpike (Overseas) Limited/EMI Music Publishing Limited.
All Rights Reserved. International Copyright Secured.

-get the sun___ in his jea-lous sky,___ as we walk in fields of gold.___

as we walk in fields of gold.___

mm,___ mm.___

mm.___

So she

So she

took her love_ for to gaze a - while up - on the fields of bar - ley. In his

So she took her love for to gaze a - while up - on the fields, fields of bar - ley.

took her love_ for to gaze a - while up - on the fields of bar - ley. In his

So she took her love for to gaze a - while up - on the fields, fields of bar - ley.

arms she fell_ as her hair came down,_ a- mong the fields of gold._

In his arms she fell, her hair came down, a - mong the fields of gold._

arms she fell_ as her hair came down,_ a -mong the fields of gold._ Will you

In his arms she fell, her hair camedown, a -mong the fields of gold._ Will you

I ne-ver made pro-mi-ses light - ly,

I ne-ver made pro-mi-ses light - ly,

I ne-ver made pro-mi-ses light - ly,

I ne-ver made pro-mi-ses light - ly,

And there have been some that I've bro - ken, but I swear in the

And there have been some that I've bro - ken, but I swear in the

And there have been some that I've bro - ken, but I swear in the

And there have been some that I've bro - ken, but I swear in the

days still left, we'll walk in fields of gold.

days still left, we'll walk in fields of gold.

days still left, we'll walk in fields of gold.

days still left, we'll walk in fields of gold.

Bm   G   A   Bm

Ma-ny years have passed

Ma-ny years have

Ma-ny years have passed since those

Ma-ny years have passed

G   D   Bm

55

since those sum- mer, a - mong the fields of bar - ley.

passed since those sum - mer days, a - mong the fields, fields of bar-ley.

sum- mer days,_ a - mong the fields of bar-ley. See the

_ since those sum - mer days,_ a -

G   D

58

See the child-ren run as the sun goes down, a - mong the fields of gold._

See the child - ren as the sun goes down, a - mong the fields of gold._

child-ren run_ as the sun goes down,_ a - mong the fields of gold._

-mong the fields of bar - ley, fields of gold.

Bm   G   D   G/B   A

HALLELUJAH

WORDS & MUSIC BY LEONARD COHEN

Arranged by Jonathan Wikeley

© Copyright 1984 Sony/ATV Music Publishing (UK) Limited.
All Rights Reserved. International Copyright Secured.

ooh, Hal-le-lu - - jah.

dim.

Hal-le-lu - jah, Hal-le-lu - jah, ooh.

ooh, ooh.

ooh, ooh.

mp

(Tenor or TB unison)

mp

Your faith was strong but you need-ed proof, you

Am   C   Am   C   Am

saw her bath - ing on the roof, her beau - ty and the moon - light o - ver-

C   Am   F   G

15

35

-threw you._____ She tied you to a kit-chen chair, she broke your throne_ and she

cresc.

C   G   C   F   E   Am

40

cut your hair,   and from your lips she drew the Hal - le - lu - jah._____ Hal - le-

dim.

F   G   Em   Am   Em/G

45 *mp*

-lu - jah,_____ Hal - le - lu - jah,_____ Hal - le - lu - jah,_____

F   F/G   Am   Am/G   F

mp

50

_____ Hal - le - lu - - - - jah.

C/G   G   C   Am

16

18

21

HERO

WORDS & MUSIC BY MARIAH CAREY & WALTER AFANASIEFF

Arranged by Jonathan Wikeley

© Copyright 1993 Rye Songs/Wally World Music, USA. Warner/Chappell Music Limited (50%)/
Universal/MCA Music Limited (50%) (administered in Germany by Universal/MCA Music Publ. GmbH).
All Rights Reserved. International Copyright Secured.

29

tear them a-way.___   Hold   on,_____   there will be to-mor-row,

tear them a-way.___   Aah,   aah.

tear them a-way.___   Aah.

tear them a-way.___   Aah.

A♭   E♭/G   Fm⁷   E♭   D♭   A♭/C   A♭   E♭

rit.   **a tempo**

in   time you'll find the   way._____

Aah.

Aah.   Then a he - ro comes a-long,_

Aah.

Aah._____

D♭   A♭/C   Csus⁴   C   G

MAKE YOU FEEL MY LOVE

WORDS & MUSIC BY BOB DYLAN

Arranged by Jeremy Birchall

This arrangement may be sung 'a cappella', without the accompaniment.

 © Copyright 1997 Special Rider Music.
All Rights Reserved. International Copyright Secured.

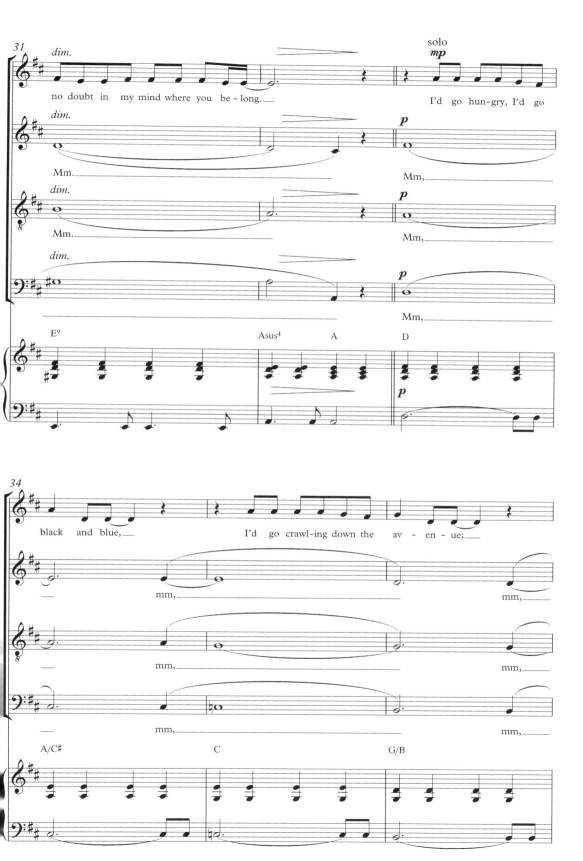

MAN IN THE MIRROR

WORDS & MUSIC BY GLEN BALLARD & SIEDAH GARRETT

Arranged by John Wikeley

© Copyright 1987 Aerostation Corporation, USA/Yellow Brick Road Music, USA. Universal/MCA Music Limited
(50%) (administered in Germany by Universal/MCA Music Publ. GmbH.)/Cherry Lane Music Limited (50%).
All Rights Reserved. International Copyright Secured.

49

50

wan-na make the world a bet - ter place take a look at your-self__ then make that

wan-na make the world a bet - ter place take a look at your-self__ then make that

wan-na make the world a bet - ter place take a look at your-self__ then make that

wan-na make the world a bet - ter place take a look at your-self__ then make that

change. I'm start-ing with the man in the mir-ror. I'm ask-ing him to

change. Man in the mir-ror, oh yeah.

change. I'm start-ing with the man in the mir-ror, oh yeah. I'm ask-ing him to

change. Man in the mir-ror, oh yeah.

add hand claps on off-beats

Change,—

Change,—

(*optional solo to end)

It's gon-na feel real good. "Sham - one!"   Just lift your-self, you know,

Change,—

(optional cut to bar 125)

yeah,   make that   change.

yeah,   make that   change.

you got to stop it   your - self.   You got-ta make that

yeah,   make that   change.

* the Tenor from 102 is a notated 'ad lib' section and could be performed by a soloist improvising
around the written part. To perform without this section, see note at bar 106.

RULE THE WORLD

WORDS & MUSIC BY MARK OWEN, GARY BARLOW, JASON ORANGE & HOWARD DONALD

Arranged by Jeremy Birchall

© Copyright 2007 EMI Music Publishing Limited (50%)/Sony/ATV Music Publishing (UK) Limited (25%)/
Universal Music Publishing Limited (25%) (administered in Germany by Universal Music Publ. GmbH).
All Rights Reserved. International Copyright Secured.

64

RUN

WORDS & MUSIC BY GARY LIGHTBODY, JONATHAN QUINN, MARK McCLELLAND,
NATHAN CONNOLLY & IAIN ARCHER
Arranged by Jeremy Birchall

© Copyright 2003 Universal Music Publishing BL Limited (95%)
(administered in Germany by Universal Music Publ. GmbH)/Kobalt Music Publishing Limited (5%).
All Rights Reserved. International Copyright Secured.

YOU RAISE ME UP

WORDS & MUSIC BY BRENDAN GRAHAM & ROLF LØVLAND

Arranged by Christopher Hussey

*Humming should sound continuous, changes of breath should be as subtle as possible.

© Copyright 2001 Universal Music AS, Norway/Peermusic (Ireland) Limited Universal-Polygram International Publishing, Inc./Alfred Publishing Company, Inc. (50%)/Peermusic (UK) Limited (50%). All Rights Reserved. International Copyright Secured.

94